MY WARMEST SORROW

PREETHI VENUGOPALA

Copyright © Preethi Venugopala
All Rights Reserved.

Contents

I said: What about my eyes?
God said: Keep them on the road.
I said: What about my passion?
God said: Keep it burning.
I said: What about my heart?
God said: Tell me what you hold inside it?
I said: Pain and sorrow?
He said: Stay with it. The wound is the place where the
Light enters you.
-Rumi

1

Jasmine

Natsukashii. A former colleague had introduced the word to me. When a feeling warmed the heart and awakened memories, the Japanese called it Natsukashii.

When I unlocked the door to my flat that Wednesday night, weary after a long day at work, I was in my Natsukashii mode as usual. The cool night breeze that caressed my cheek through the open window, as the cab traversed the lanes of Bangalore, had a way of switching that mode on.

After all, it had begun here. The warmth that had blossomed inside a twenty-two-year old's heart five years ago. Except during these brief sojourns into the past, my day-to-day existence was like a cold, placid lake, slowly dying from within.

Little did I know that within the next thirty minutes or so, a dormant volcano would spew lava into it, awakening a world of unexpected warmth.

As the project deadline was looming near, I'd remained in the office till nine to complete the chunk of work scheduled for the day. Structural designing demanded full dedication, even for a small-scale project. And my current project was unbelievably complex.

Just as I slumped onto the couch, my mobile started ringing. I ignored it. I was in no mood to talk to anyone. Even though there wasn't a dearth of people who wanted to give me company, I felt alone. In fact, I was beginning to like loneliness. Solitude wasn't scary anymore. I didn't know if it was a good thing or a bad thing. But as far as I knew, I needed these hours of silence and the absence of human connection to remain sane.

It soon became evident that whoever was calling wasn't in a mood to grant me my moments of peace. When it rang for the third time in the next five minutes, I sighed in defeat and rummaged in my bag to locate it.

"Jasmine, you won't believe what happened today. And, where were you? I called you so many times," shrieked Ashima, the moment I answered the phone.

I rolled my eyes but a smile curved my lips. Ashima, my engineering classmate, had a flair for theatrics. What was it now?

"Slow down. I just returned home after a gruelling day. We have a deadline this Saturday."

"Eek. Be like me and find a government job. The perks of a government job are endless. Private jobs suck, " said Ashima.

"Now, now... you've to go to that magnificent job tomorrow, right? Why are you staying up late?"

Ashima had been like our dorm room alarm while in college. She dozed off exactly at nine and got up at five in the morning, every day, without fail. What had kept her awake today? Or had her so-called relaxing job altered her lifestyle?

"Idiot, check your WhatsApp messages. I don't want to spoil the surprise. Thank me later. Goodnight for now."

No! Not again. Mostly, she called me for additional support when she was on the verge of losing some debate she had initiated in our group. Who was she arguing with today? Rahul or Avinash?

Most of my classmates were politically active. Every new government decision or policy would undergo a detailed post-mortem inside our class WhatsApp group. Rahul was a devout follower of the Congress party, Avinash was a self-confessed Modi *Bhakt* and Ashima was a red comrade entirely. On some days, their debates would continue for days. I didn't have the energy to jump into another nonsensical discussion. All I craved now was food. And after that to sleep till the alarm rang at seven tomorrow morning.

I switched on the geyser to take a quick bath. Then I transferred the *biryani* I had bought into a plate and placed it into the oven to reheat it. In the present Bangalore climate, nothing stayed warm for long. I was not fond of the winters. It wasn't the cold that bothered me, though. The winter season brought back long-lost memories, making me long for the warmth of a specific loving embrace. It also reminded me of my twenty-two-year-old self who had almost given up on life.

By the time I returned from the bath, there were two more missed calls from Ashima. What was wrong with this girl today?

As I dug into the tasty *biryani*, I turned on my phone data. Notification beeps began. I swiped left till I found the WhatsApp icon. I had 1200 plus unread messages just from the Civil Gang 2013, my class WhatsApp group. Some serious discussion must be happening. I groaned inwardly. I wasn't in the mood to drown in nasty arguments. But Ashima would probably kill me if I didn't hop in and speak my bit.

Avinash and Ashima had sent me private messages as well. What was so urgent?

Curious, I opened the group chat. Avinash had added a new member this evening. Though our class had a total strength of 60 students, there were only 45 members in the group currently. Many of my former classmates were pursuing higher studies whereas some had landed jobs in distant lands. Hence, we had lost contact with many of them in the five years that had elapsed after graduation. Occasionally, a new member would be found and added by one of the admins. Then there would be a mad rush to get reacquainted with the new entrant.

The name of the person added today drove away all my lethargy in a flash. I blinked twice to confirm if I had correctly read the name mentioned in Avinash's welcoming message.

Ajay Menon. Ajay... after all these years?

A warm sorrow enveloped my heart and it began to struggle like a caged bird. It became difficult to breathe. Letters blurred as my eyes brimmed with tears. The phone slipped out of my hand and fell onto the couch. I got up and ran towards the French windows that opened to the balcony.

Pushing the panels open, I breathed in the fresh air wafting in from the garden that flanked our company apartment complex on all four sides. This tiny lung space amid the vast concrete jungle that was the apartment complex helped me keep some of my very cherished memories alive.

Memories that my parents had asked me to bury. Memories that often choked me and kept me awake during dreary, wintry nights.

How many shocks lay in store for me in the thousand unread messages that awaited me?

A part of me ached to know more about the one person who had been my whole world all those years ago.

All those years ago? Who was I kidding? Ajay still owned my heart. Entirely. Every single thought was torture or a pleasure depending on his absence or presence in it. Had I manifested him back in my life via my obsessive thoughts?

Sheela, my counsellor, often advised me to let bygones be bygones and move on. But had the stoic bespectacled woman ever known love? Perhaps. But probably the kind of love she knew was unlike the one that ruled my heart. If she had known such a love, she wouldn't have asked me to let go of Ajay's memories. How could one let go of something that was imprinted right into one's soul?

Breathe deep, Jasmine. You can face this, I told myself. Five years were enough to change a person entirely. I'd changed, hadn't I? I was no longer the person whose life decisions were made by her parents. I hadn't even seen them in years. Mom often called me but I never answered her calls. By answering them, I would be exposing her to Dad's wrath. Hadn't he forbidden her to contact me?

"We don't have a daughter anymore. She died the moment she put us through all that humiliation. This is the payback we received for twenty-two years of unconditional love," he had declared on the day I'd gone against his decision for the first time.

I had wanted to hurt him badly and hence had disgraced him in front of the whole society. But the one who lost everything that day had been me.

On that torturous night, when calls to Ajay failed to connect, I realized I was alone in this world. Mom's muffled sobs from her room kept me awake, taunting me about my insane action. By the time dawn had peeked in, I'd decided it was enough.

If my younger brother Sam hadn't seen me walk out of the house in the wee hours of the morning, perhaps I wouldn't be alive today.

I don't remember what I'd been thinking when I darted out of my home in the clothes I'd worn to bed. I don't remember the path I'd taken to reach the bridge on the village border. I only remember the overpowering need to escape the despair that had conquered me. I'd wanted freedom from the hefty burden of a million 'what if' and 'why me' questions that were plaguing me.

Sam had followed me silently. When the depths of the river had beckoned me, he had sobbed, firmly catching me by the waist, entreating me to get down from the concrete barrier on the bridge.

"This is not how your story should end, Jazz. Please. Come with me. Please. Do not do this. I am with you. Let me help you."

Sheela often said that every person on the verge of suicide would turn back and smile at life if one single act of kindness touched his or her soul in that final moment. I agree. For me, Sam had been my saviour.

That near encounter with death changed me. Sam became my pillar of support and protective armour at home. For the first time, he raised his voice at Dad. He helped me search for jobs online and fill in job applications. It was my sibling who unclipped my wings.

Once I soared with my new wings, I decided not to let my love for one person make me forget everyone else. I decided to embrace life one more time. This job had become a life saviour. The many deadlines and demanding work schedules made me get over most of the emotional trauma.

Most importantly, it had given me the anonymity I craved. Here, I wasn't greeted by teasing glances or sniggers, nor were hurtful words hurled at me heartlessly.

Bengaluru had embraced me with open arms. It had become my haven. I'd learned to be independent but had become a loner. I had no social life to talk about. All my interactions had been limited to online chats with a few friends who acted as though we were still in college. And who took care to not remind me of the blackest phase of my life.

I inhaled a few more lungfuls of the cold night air and returned to the couch. The phone was blinking with notifications. Really, these guys were jobless.

But I could understand their enthusiasm. Ajay had been the soul of our class. His mere presence had made the class come alive. Not only had he been brilliant academically, but also active in extracurricular activities. More than that, he had been the kindest human being on campus.

It was our limitless enthusiasm for studies that had brought us close. We were lab partners who could find a solution to any problem that crossed our path. Long hours finding a solution for complex structural problems and then helping others crack them as well had become our thing. Mostly, we would have a bunch of classmates surrounding us during the study holidays for university exams.

We didn't know exactly when our friendship began to change colours. We were in deep by the time realization struck. Even though we were convinced we were the perfect pair, the world outside our campus looked at us through tinted glasses. Our religion, financial and societal status were all total mismatches. My father was a Superintendent of Police whereas Ajay's parents were teachers at a government high school. We were Roman Catholics whereas Ajay belonged to an orthodox Hindu family.

I was the first one to give up.

I didn't think our love was strong enough to stand the onslaught of hatred and threats from my Dad.

It had only taken moments for me to realize that our love could spell doom to Ajay's life. After what had happened that day years ago. After my father had revealed what he could and would do to Ajay if I went against his wishes. Perhaps he knew I valued Ajay's life more than our togetherness.

My mother's failing health was perhaps another reason.

I was the one who decided to end my relationship with Ajay. We met for the last time on our graduation day.

"Don't you think we deserve to live the life we want? Are we not adults now? Can't we decide how we want to live our life?"

Ajay's words had made me cry inwardly but I'd acted as if I didn't care. I told him there existed no future for us. Whatever we had experienced in that past year had perhaps been just an illusion.

In a way, it had been. It had been a reality only for us. On my insistence, we hadn't even shared our secret with our best friends. No one knew that our friendship had blossomed into love.

I'd laid out reasons to prove we wouldn't work.

Wouldn't we regret our decision if we went against our parents to fulfil our desires?

Wouldn't such a regret snuff out the flame of love inside our hearts?

I'd argued vehemently, hiding the real reason I was being forced to leave him behind a wall of words. If I had told him about the threats issued by my father, he would have laughed it off.

When I walked away from him that day, I had resigned myself to my colourless fate. I had made my choice. But I had misunderstood the power of obsessive love. I had underestimated the depth to which I loved Ajay. It had been too late to turn back by the time I understood it.

I took my phone and unlocked it. Exhaling deeply, I scrolled to Avinash's welcome message. Ajay had replied immediately:

AJAY: Hello guys, I am thrilled to meet you all again. Though virtually.

Others had jumped in to greet him and had begun enquiries.

RAHUL: Where the hell had you been, man? Five years!! How could anyone go MIA just like that?

PRIYA: How are you, dear? Do post some latest pics. We missed you so much.

Priya's message slightly irritated me. *How are you, dear?* She used to have a Himalayan crush on Ajay since the beginning of our course. Was it just me or did her infatuation resurface after all these years? Her follow-up questions continued to irritate me.

PRIYA: Are you there on Facebook? Can I add you?

PRIYA: Are you married?

PRIYA: Where are you working?

The questions were pouring in. Not only from her but from many others as well.

Ajay appeared his usual cheery self. He had posted replies to all the questions. I scrolled down concentrating on his answers alone.

AJAY: Guys, guys, patience. I will answer all of your questions. I am fine. I was living and working in Delhi till now. And I am sorry for not keeping in touch with any

of you all these years. Work was intense. I changed fields recently. Got selected into the Indian Administrative Service. Waiting to be posted.

Several 'oh, awesome', 'congratulations', 'proud of you' messages followed his answer.

Priya's next message reeked of regret.

PRIYA: IAS?!!!!! OMG. Who would've thought?

Back then, she used to hover around Ajay all the time like a disgusting house fly. Ashima had even named her DQB, acronym for Disgusting Queen Bee. Priya had indeed then been Ajay's biggest fan. But her overt displays of affection hadn't succeeded in winning over Ajay then. Even now, post two kids and a four-year-long marriage, she still seemed determined to get into Ajay's good books.

She and a few others were bombarding Ajay with questions. And Ajay was patiently answering them and asking questions too.

AJAY: How are you all? And what are you all doing these days? Tell me. I am all ears. I am checking all your profile pics. Some of you have become unrecognisable.

ASHIMA: Yup. People like me grew. Horizontally sadly. Except for Jasmine. She has somehow managed to stop time. Maybe it is because she is now settled in Bangalore, the garden city. Who can grow old there?

Ashima liked to exaggerate! As if I hadn't changed. I hardly enjoyed food these days, my eyes had dark circles prominently and my heart ached constantly as if it was bound by barbed wire chains. Involuntarily I checked my profile pic. It seemed decent.

Now that I remembered, Sam, who had taken the photo three months ago, had asked me to smile while thinking about someone I loved.

"That way your eyes will light up," he had suggested. Automatically, I had thought of Ajay. When he showed me the photo, I loved it. It showed glimpses of that twenty-two-year-old self who still believed that life was full of rainbows.

And then Priya asked Ajay again if he was married. My heart started racing as I read his answer.

AJAY: Not yet. But I am in a relationship. We met at the academy. Her name is Anjali.

My heart sank. Anjali! He had found someone. I didn't matter to him anymore. My Ajay was not mine now.

Automatically, my hands moved to turn off the mobile data. Tears blurred my vision. Wasn't this what I deserved? Maybe this was what they called Karma. You received what you gave.

I believe God wrote only sadness in my destiny.

2

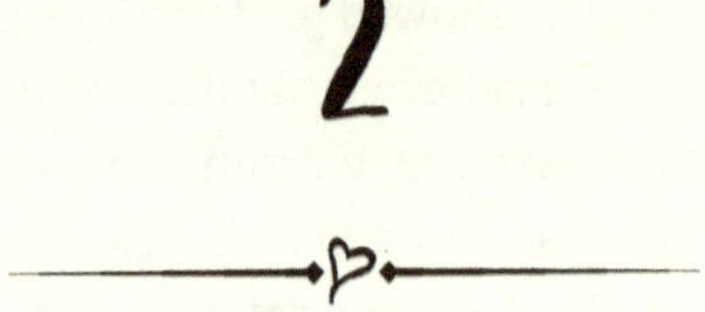

Ajay

Jasmine had been online for the last hour. I'd checked her last seen almost every hour obsessively. But she had gone offline without even writing a welcome message in the group. I had, in fact, hoped that she might send me a personal message. I felt crushed. No reaction from her even after reading about Anjali. Married life had certainly changed her.

I don't know if meeting Avinash at the Delhi airport this evening had been a stroke of good luck or bad luck. We had talked for just five minutes, but we had exchanged numbers. The next thing I know, I was added to the class WhatsApp group.

My first instinct had been to quit. For sure, I would not be able to spend time chatting with friends once I joined work. I would be inundated with work. But the enthusiastic welcome of my former classmates and the humongous yearning to hear from Jasmine had made me stay put.

Even hours after I joined, Jasmine hadn't come online. Why I had saved her profile picture, I have no idea. Perhaps, old habits die hard. I still treasured all the pictures of us together. Even after I had decided to let go of the past and chase a happy, unappealing future, I couldn't get myself to part with her photos. They were safe and secure in my cupboard at home in an album hidden at the bottom of an old trunk. Whenever memories came hunting, I pulled out the old trunk and dived into those memories. I wished I could do the same now. But here, in Mussoorie, all I owned were books and clothes.

I turned to WhatsApp again and reread the one paragraph Ashima had written about Jasmine. To my dismay, she hadn't mentioned if she had any kids yet. The only info was that she was now settled in Bangalore and worked in an international structural design firm.

Bangalore! Was God throwing me again into her path? My first appointment after training was to be in Bangalore as Sub Divisional Magistrate (SDM).

At the time when I put down my options, it had seemed like a neutral place. I hadn't given Kerala as my first option because I didn't want to run into old acquaintances. Especially, I didn't want to be anywhere near Jasmine. Jacob worked in Kochi.

It had taken me years to forget her betrayal. I had quit my job and travelled the world after working for a year, looking for solace in strange places and people. I hadn't even called home or kept in touch with my family regularly. But they knew, especially my mother, that I needed that break.

After a quick trip through Europe, I had finally settled in Bali for a while. It was during that time that I began dreaming of becoming an IAS officer. All thanks to my new friend, Rajneesh, a Malayalee Indian Foreign Service officer, who worked at the Indian embassy in Bali. Like me, he had been a civil engineer and he had become my guide. My initial aim was to opt for IFS and settle away from

India just like him. India still held painful memories. When the results of the Civil Services examinations came, I was among the top 100 in the country. When he questioned my reluctance about joining the IAS, I had told him the reason.

"Don't let the past become your burden. It has already happened, right? Let it go. Build a bright future instead by accepting what God has bestowed on you. IAS is a dream, not many achieve. *Carpe Diem*, mate," he'd said.

From then on, I'd begun to consciously give attention to my present and future instead of a long-gone past that was giving me nothing but pain. Even though the urge to dig for information about Jasmine or search for her presence on social media raised its head quite often, I forced myself to fight the temptation.

And yet, here I was. Again, chasing after her. Being ignored by her even after my vain attempt to show what I had become and how I had moved on.

Or was it mention of Anjali that brought on the silent treatment?

How would she react if she knew that Anjali was a figment of my imagination?

I'd created Anjali out of thin air. I'd been talking to my mother one day and she told me she had begun searching for a bride for me. I wasn't ready for marriage. So, I'd lied that I'd fallen in love with a fellow trainee at the institute.

"What is her name? Where is she from?"

I'd uttered the first name that came to my mind. Anjali, perhaps because 'Kuch Kuch Hota hai' was the movie I watched on Amazon Prime whenever I felt like it. Something about the magic of second chances made me sit through the three-hour-long dance, song and drama every time. Or perhaps it was because the main character's mannerisms, her attitude about friendship and love reminded me of Jasmine. Every single time, I rooted for Anjali. I could relate to her. My first love too was unrequited.

Anjali was my imaginary lover, my replacement for Jasmine. Mother had stopped bothering me after that. It had come easily, hence, when the guys in the group had asked about my girlfriend. Talking about Anjali had been easy. My ulterior motive had been to see how Jasmine would react. But she hadn't responded at all. So much for the effort.

Maybe I should find an Anjali for myself. Maybe this group would do me good. It would tell me what I was doing was wrong. I should quit yearning for my unrequited love.

No one in the group had married classmates. I remember there were at least six couples in our class who acted as if they were soulmates. As far as I could see, none of them was together now. Some had broken up while in the final year and some had gone separate ways after the course ended.

No one knew our love story. We had been good friends from the first year and that was how we were known until our course ended. It was Jasmine who had wanted to keep our relationship a secret.

The result was that the people in the group talked to me about Jasmine casually. If they knew how much pain they were giving me by mentioning my old lover, they might not have said a word. But somehow, I welcomed that pain. I was ready to torture myself more.

Jasmine had been the best thing that had happened to me. She had been the first classmate I had met. When we became good friends, my heart had jumped from friendship to love quite easily. It was hard not to fall in love with her. Beauty combined with a sharp brain. A loving human being and a loyal friend, Jasmine had become my everything very soon.

She had taken time to fall in love. But once we were in love, it had been like being immersed in an ethereal fire. It transformed me and ignited my soul. My every dream catered to the requirements of another individual, who was like God to me. The need to do well in life had become a passion. We had woven dreams together.

And then... she trashed all our dreams and found happiness elsewhere. In doing so, she had killed me, together with my hopes and dreams.

Yet, even now every cell in my body pulsed with a different sort of energy at the mere mention of her name. Would I ever be able to forget her?

The antique clock on the wall chimed five times. I hadn't slept a wink. The night that had passed had felt eerily like how it had been during my wanderlust year.

Heart heavy with regret and sadness and the constant thought that I would never be happy again. If this was how it was even before I heard from her, how would it be if we actually interacted? Or met?

Would I be able to breathe normally again? Would I get closure?

3

Jasmine

I woke up the next morning with a blinding headache. My whole body tingled as though I had ingested something toxic. Was I coming down with a fever?

I threw aside the blanket and walked toward the bedroom balcony. And it all came back. Every single dream that had played out in my mind yesterday night. My dreams were still better than my reality. Because, in them, I had been with Ajay. We had been living in a sweet little home that looked like something straight out of a fairy tale. We had pretty babies. We had made love all night and still couldn't get enough of each other.

Pathetic. How could I make this stop?

I must make it stop. What good would it do to dwell on such dreams?

How could I stop this yearning?

How could I stop myself from spending endless nights staring at the ceiling wishing I could talk to him?

I had stopped myself multiple times from pressing the call button on the number listed against his name yesterday. I had to stop this madness.

It was time to visit Sheela.

Dr Sheela Mehta was my counsellor and friend. Every time I had a relapse of these painful episodes of relentless dreams and restlessness, which was often, I sought Sheela's guidance.

We had met at the yoga and meditation class. I had attended the class to seek a way to control my repetitive thoughts and had struck up a friendship with Sheela very soon. And the best part was she lived in the opposite apartment complex.

"Can I come in today before office?" I asked when Sheela picked up the phone.

"Yes. Come any time before nine. The kids and Sumeet have left."

I poured some mango juice for myself before rushing off to Sheela's home.

Sheela opened the door with a smile and welcomed me with a warm hug. She silently guided me to the tiny spare bedroom that she'd equipped for private consultations.

"He is back," I blurted out the moment I sat down on the comfortable chair across from her.

To anyone else, those words might not have made sense. But between Sheela and me, there were no secrets. She knew me better than anyone in the world.

Yet, Sheela wrinkled her brow. "Isn't that what you wanted?"

"Yes. No... Exactly. I mean, that's not what I meant. Actually, I don't know why I feel this miserable. This was to be expected, right?" I mumbled as more nonsensical sentences stumbled out of my mouth. I trembled inwardly and gripped the chair handle urging myself to calm down.

"Calm down, Jasmine. Breathe in deep. Now slowing let it out. Repeat with me."

After a while, I calmed down enough to narrate what had happened.

"Ajay was added into our class WhatsApp group yesterday." I paused as I struggled to calm myself down.

"And..."

"He is in a relationship," I managed to say as I twiddled my thumbs.

"I understand what you are going through," she said, after a long minute of silence.

Her calm statement unleashed all the frustration that had been building up inside me since yesterday night.

"No, you don't understand. You can't. Have you ever spent years yearning for someone and then discovered that it was a total waste? Have you wondered whether you had got it all wrong in the first place? How can he haunt my dreams for so long if there was nothing? It felt so real. Every damn day. I can't get rid of these thoughts even if I try hard, whereas he has moved on so easily. I never gave myself a chance to fall in love with another person. I closed the door that led to my heart, locked it forever and threw away the damn keys. And see how quickly he has moved on." I exploded.

"That's life, Jasmine. People change. We've to face it. I've been telling you for years to let him go. You put an end to your relationship once. Do it again. All this while, subconsciously, you were waiting for him to come. You never stopped hoping. And hope can be a very debilitating thing when shattered. It pierces the very soul."

Then she made me talk by asking prodding questions to empty all the resentment that had been brewing inside me. By the time I left her home an hour later, I was able to breathe normally again. She gave me a CD of a new guided meditation that I was to use just before going to sleep. I was also asked to dump all my frustrations into my diary before sleeping.

After reaching home, I checked my WhatsApp messages. Ashima had messaged.

What happened? Aren't you thrilled that Ajay has returned? Or are you guys going to continue with whatever issue you had with each other? You didn't even send him a welcome message.

I wished it was just a fight. I wanted to tell her that Ajay had been more than my best friend. To curtail the barrage of questions that might follow, I replied.

I fell asleep reading the messages. Sorry. Will message him today.

I opened our group chat and typed in a welcome message to Ajay. By the time I turned off the mobile data on entering my office cabin, a few others had typed in their welcome messages as well. I had refrained from sending a personal message. Messages in the group were better. Formal and they won't turn personal.

I tuned out everything and immersed myself in work till the clock struck eight. I had dinner at the office itself before catching a cab home.

On entering my flat, I turned on my mobile data. There were plenty of new messages in our WhatsApp group again. I opened the chat eagerly. A political debate was raging with Ajay leading the discussion. I scrolled up to see his reply to my message. He had replied to everyone else but had chosen not to reply to my message.

If he was planning to play it this way, let him. I turned off my mobile data and opened my laptop to finish the work that I had brought home. Yet disappointment and anger continued to vex me.

When it all became too much, I grabbed my diary, turned on the timer for twenty minutes and began to free write as Sheela had suggested. Every single worry, every single thought that had been hovering in my mind got dumped into the blank pages. Once the timer went off, I put the journal back into my drawer. I placed Sheela's guided meditation CD into my DVD player and allowed Sheela's calming voice to guide me into a calm, blissful state. Tears raced down my cheeks during the final stages as she asked me to recollect the good moments in my life. Every cheerful memory had Ajay's face in it. Was this even a good idea? Yet, by the time the session ended, I was feeling calm unlike before. And drowsy as well.

I called Sheela to tell her how it went. I also told her what happened in the group.

"Stay away from WhatsApp till you can get yourself to admit that he has moved on. It is time to stop obsessing over him," she told me firmly.

After disconnecting her call, I stared at the phone screen for the longest time. Then I pressed my index finger on the WhatsApp icon and clicked the small X symbol that popped up.

"Are you sure you want to uninstall this app?" came the question.

Though my finger hovered over the cancel option for a while, I finally clicked 'Yes'.

4

Ajay

JASMINE: 'Welcome to the group, Ajay!'

I fumed as I reread her welcome message for the nth time. It hurt to see such a casual message from her. I'd chosen to ignore the message in the hope that she would call me out for not replying to her message.

The Jasmine I knew would've done that. But this new version of my Jasmine didn't care if I responded to her message or not. She was perhaps at this moment making love to her husband. And here I was, wallowing in self-pity. I wish I could unburden this on someone. I wished Anjali was real.

I had immersed myself into useless political ramblings just to distract myself and not go pining after her and not send whiny direct messages to her. I hadn't messaged her just because I knew I wouldn't be able to maintain the facade of normalcy and would have blurted out how much I missed her.

I clicked on her name to check on her. Her 'last seen' was still the same. Three days ago. She was still away from WhatsApp. Wouldn't she return? The scenario seemed too painful to even consider. Why was I behaving like a

teenager suffering from the first pangs of love?

Yet, every other hour in the next few days, I checked if she was back. I was back in Kerala to spend a few days with my family before I officially took charge in Bangalore. Being in the same room where I'd spent hours talking on the phone with Jasmine was proving to be hard.

On the second night, I had a strange dream. In it, I watched Jasmine kiss a faceless man while I stood staring at them from a distance. Every time she kissed him, she would eye me. Pressing herself against her husband, she had begun to moan as the faceless man caressed her curves.

I woke up with a gasp, unable to breathe. The room seemed to be closing in on me. Nameless fears and emotions were choking me. I grabbed my blanket and pillow and escaped to my sister's old bedroom downstairs. In the morning, when my mother found me there, I made the excuse that there were too many mosquitoes in my room. My mother's face told me she didn't believe me. But much to my relief, she didn't prod further.

Days passed by without any news from Jasmine. Unable to hold it in anymore, I texted Avinash and Ashima asking if anything was wrong with Jasmine. Both Avinash and Ashima believed it was nothing. Jasmine was always a bit moody these days. They wouldn't tell anything much about her even though I tried hard to drag our private chats back towards Jasmine. Mostly, whenever I mentioned Jasmine, both would flip the topic casually to something else or dismiss my question without a proper answer. Was Jasmine not happy in her marriage? Was her husband a heartless bastard?

That Saturday morning, half-heartedly I went with my mother to a *Satsang* organised by our community. I had expected to get bored there. But when the Guru began to speak, I was mesmerised by the truth and practicality of his wise words. One lesson stayed put in my mind.

"Romantic love is an emotion that our ego generates to keep us under its control. Why do you look outside of yourself to find true love? True love lies within you. Do not seek love outside of yourselves. When you allow yourselves to pine after a person who has given you pain, who are you not loving? When you pin your happiness on the actions or validation from another individual, you are undervaluing your own magnificence. Each one of us is the child of God. Let your own light shine. Do not dim it for anyone. Each one of us is responsible for our own happiness. Make yourself the priority in your life. People don't value coal. They value diamonds, even though both are made of carbon. Decide what you want to be. Shine like a diamond by being your magnificent self. Don't be coal and waste your time and energy pining after a past trauma or a person who has given you pain."

His words rang in my mind that whole day.

It was time to move on.

I should let Jasmine go.

I shouldn't pin my hopes on her.

Jasmine was no longer mine. She had her own family.

I should stop torturing myself over an impossible dream.

It was with that determination that I opened my WhatsApp chat group that day. Remembering the Guru's words, I stopped myself from checking if Jasmine was back. I just focussed on the ones who were interested to talk to me and that felt kind of relaxing for the first time.

It felt amazing when I finally let go of the burden of the expectations I had carried with me like a heavy backpack. In my onward journey, I was going to let go. I had to let go of my past self and embrace my future self.

5

Jasmine

By that weekend, I put an end to two things. My current project and my time away from WhatsApp. I reinstalled the app because of two reasons.

First was Ashima's relentless threats. She wanted me to end whatever issue I had with Ajay. The second was my eagerness to hear from Ajay.

The fear that had held me back from Ajay five years ago had waned through the years, especially after my father's retirement. He was now just an old lion with very bad teeth. Even his so-called roar didn't faze me anymore.

But sadly, now there was another person that stood between me and Ajay. Anjali. Someone who suited him in every way.

The sane voice inside me hissed in my ears. "Forget it, Jasmine. Anjali, being an IAS officer is a better match for Ajay. She knows his world better than you."

A small voice inside me protested. "I know Ajay more."
Really? Did I?

All through the week, I'd hoped Ajay would call or message when I continued to remain away from the group. But he hadn't. It was clear. He didn't care.

Often during the week, I reminisced about the kind of attention he used to shower on me while in college. Instead of helping me forget him through journaling and meditation, my stubborn heart made me relive our love story daily.

I still remember the first time I had seen Ajay. It seemed like we were destined to be together right from the beginning. On the first day of college, I'd been waiting with my father to see our department head to officially get inducted into the course. I had to fill in several applications and submit my certificates. In my hurry, I'd forgotten to take a pen.

"Is this how you're going to be a professional? How can you be so irresponsible?" Dad had begun lecturing me right there in the hall in front of 20 or more students along with their parents in his booming voice.

Wherever there was a crowd, he loved to prove that he was a strict parent. That meant we were regularly scolded publicly. According to him, we were utter failures. I had chosen engineering when he had wanted me to take up medicine. Also, being the Superintendent of Police meant that everywhere he went, people treated him with respect. No one ever took our side.

I was shrinking more and more into my shell as Dad continued his lecturing. Then, someone slipped a pen onto my desk. It was the boy who sat behind me.

"Keep it. I have completed all the formalities. I don't need it now. See you in class."

That timely help had been Ajay's first act of kindness towards me. Throughout the four years in college, he hardly ever got angry with me or anyone else. It had been impossible to not like him. We had become the best of friends within no time.

Though we spent most of our waking hours together, our relationship had never crossed the boundaries of friendship until the college tour in the sixth semester. By then, many of our classmates had found lovers within the class itself. Only a few of us were still unattached. That day, as the bus plodded through the hilly terrain of the Western ghats, several of the seats were occupied by couples. Ajay sat next to me and we had talked about random things. Romance had been the last thing on my mind then.

Sometime that night, I fell asleep listening to him speak. When I woke up, I was leaning on his shoulder and he was fast asleep. Perhaps I had been sleeping all night on his shoulder. He had also wrapped his blanket around me to keep me warm whereas he was wearing just a thin jacket. It was at that moment when I had looked at his dear face up close, that I first realised that I loved him. I had spent the rest of the night just gazing at him every now and then, as he continued to sleep, and blush for no reason.

The feeling had continued to grow all night. It had become so intense that I started to avoid being near him the next day. Whenever he came to sit near me, I made excuses and went and sat with somebody else. It was becoming too hard to resist the attraction I felt. It felt scary as hell. I didn't want to lose his friendship just because my heart was misbehaving.

But he noticed the change in my behaviour. He cornered me when we were visiting Tipu Sultan's summer palace in Bangalore. Ashima, who had been with me till then, had gone in search of a washroom. I had been waiting for her in a deserted corridor, reading a book and resting my tired limbs.

"What's it, Jasmine? What's wrong? Why are you avoiding me?"

"I am not. You are imagining things," I said. Yet when his intense black eyes searched my face, I blushed and turned away.

"Don't, Jasmine. Tell me. I have this disgusting habit of talking in my sleep. Did I say something to upset you?"

That question intrigued me. What was he hiding? Just to test him, I said, "Yes, you did. I didn't expect this from you."

"Sorry, Jasmine. I couldn't help it. The heart has its way. Aren't we all slaves to our hearts? It's always been you. I should've told you before. I love you so much but I didn't want to risk losing our friendship."

I cannot explain the joy his words had given me then. I'd leapt onto him like a happy child and hugged him tight and exclaimed.

"I love you too! It took me so long to realize it. I'm an idiot."

His face had lit up and his arms had chained me to him. He pulled me into an alcove and slowly and tenderly claimed my lips. I had never believed it when romances had called kisses magical. But his kisses proved me wrong. How had I lived till then without experiencing such magical moments?

After that, it became hard for us to not be together. For the next two days, we visited some of the many quaint and beautiful spots in Karnataka including many ancient temples and trekked to explore some magnificent viewpoints.

On the second morning, our group visited the famed Nandi hills to watch the sunrise from its famed viewpoint. As it was extremely cold, we had all huddled together on the rock at the top of the hill, waiting for the sun to rise. Ajay had dragged me to sit beside him towards the edge of our group. As the sun rose magnificently from a bed of fluffy white clouds, we all cheered and whistled entranced by the magnificence of it all. At the same moment, I felt Ajay lean closer and whisper 'I love you' in my ear. Then silently, he had slipped a thin silver ring that had two cute entwined hearts onto my left ring finger. I loved it on sight.

"Saw this and it reminded me of us. It is a promise ring. I picked it up from one of the local stores yesterday," Ajay said in a soft voice. Ah! So that was why he had vanished the previous night after we had stopped for the day at the hotel. I had kissed the ring and squeezed his hand in gratitude. The world had suddenly become a lot brighter and happier.

When we returned to the bus after that, I regretted it when Ashima insisted that I sit next to her. Ajay seemed disappointed as well. Later, when I got the chance, I shopped for a promise ring for Ajay. I chose a plain silver band with 'My heart is yours' engraved in loopy letters on the inner side. I still remember how he had grinned like a happy child when I slipped it on his finger that night. We had met for a short walk after dinner in the garden of the hotel we were staying at. I also remember the searing kisses that he had planted on my lips.

The next two days added many more colourful memories to our love story. Each place became memorable for one or the other reason. Each memory had our happy faces etched on it. It felt like our hearts would break when the tour ended.

We hadn't canoodled enough.

We hadn't talked enough.

We hadn't roamed enough.

Unlike the tours from previous years, I didn't even look forward to being back in the hostel and sleeping for a whole day to rest my tired limbs. We didn't want to part and go to different hostels. But we had to.

Because I feared my father's wrath, we had decided to keep our relationship a secret. We didn't want him to hear about us from one of his spies inside the college who were ordered to keep an eye on me. It was difficult to act normal when all we wanted was to be in each other's arms. One weekend before the final exams, we decided to take our relationship a step further.

We took a short trip on Ajay's bike to a nearby hill station and spent the weekend there.

The tiny resort in Coorg we went to was chosen carefully. The one thing it granted us was privacy. The old couple who owned it had handed us the keys and walked off to their home on the other side of the hill.

We had the entire place to ourselves. Food would magically appear at the doorstep counter during meal times. Happy to be left alone for the first time, all we did was satisfy our thirst for each other. We made love, talked about our happy future and made love again.

The magic ended too soon and rather abruptly.

My father, who had come to visit me at the hostel to check on me, was furious when he found me missing. He used all his official powers to locate us. Ajay was arrested on his orders from the resort. He slapped me as Ajay was being dragged into the police van. Then he had threatened to ruin him when I had tried to run towards Ajay.

"He won't come out once he goes in. Don't you dare humiliate me!"

He warned me again when I declared that I loved Ajay and would marry only him.

"Forget him and he will live. Else, you will soon hear about a college student who committed suicide inside a jail cell."

I knew enough about my father to understand that it was not a hollow threat. I had given in and promised to forget Ajay. Ajay's life was more precious than our togetherness.

But I had determined to find a way to exact revenge on my father. In the end, nothing mattered. Because I had lost Ajay by then.

6

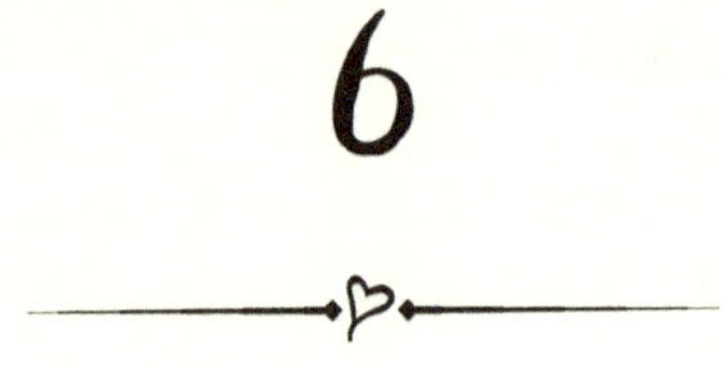

Ajay

I couldn't forget her. That much was clear. After listening to the Guru at the Satsang, I'd decided to let go of Jasmine's memories. I'd taken out the album from my cupboard that night intending to burn the photos. But instead, those remnants from our time together had pulled me back into those golden moments of togetherness. I couldn't bring myself to burn them.

Among the photos, the photo that affected me the most had been taken during our graduation ceremony.

I looked elated but Jasmine looked as if on the verge of tears. Now I could understand why. At that moment I hadn't a clue that minutes later she would break up with me and hand me the invitation to her wedding. I'd been happy that I had finally seen her. We hadn't even talked since the day her father had caught us both together.

It had been a humiliating experience. When I had been hauled into the police jeep, I had watched a teary Jasmine getting into their car with her father. When the police had let me off with a warning, I'd thought Jasmine had found a way to convince her father about us. How wrong I had been.

I clearly remember that fateful afternoon that had been the last time we met. Right after the graduation photos were clicked, I dragged her to our favourite nook in the college—the garden bench under the shadowed canopy of the Gulmohar tree. Called the lovers' corner, the bench was a sought-after spot for all the Romeos and Juliets on the campus. The decorative bushes that surrounded it provided privacy and the beautiful garden on the other side was a pleasure to behold.

Holding her within the circle of my arms that day had filled me with a sense of contentment. She had protested that we shouldn't. It was not the right time; her parents were inside the campus. I hadn't listened. I needed to touch her. To kiss her. In the last few days, I hadn't even heard her sweet voice.

Once away from prying eyes around, I had pulled her into a tight hug. Being away from her had felt like being exiled from everything I held dear. Cupping her face, I pressed my mouth to Jasmine's. Heat exploded the moment our lips touched. She had responded by parting her lips and angling them better to receive and return my kisses. And then, when my hands had begun to wander to caress her lush curves, she had stiffened. Stopping my errant hands, she moved to the other corner of the bench. When I scooted closer, she turned to me with eyes brimming with tears.

"I can't do this, Ajay. It is wrong," she had said, fidgeting with the promise ring I had given her.

"Wrong? We have promised to be each other's forever, darling. This is not wrong."

"Wait. I have to show you this."

Wiping her tears, she had pulled out a fancy envelope that seemed like a wedding invitation. Dread had crept into my heart.

"I have consented to marry the one my family has chosen for me. Jacob Augustine is their choice. He is an accountant with an MNC in Kochi."

Her words had fallen like hot lava on me. Unable to believe what I was hearing, I knelt in front of her and grabbed her hands. Squeezing them, I repeatedly begged her to tell me she was joking.

She had shaken her head.

"I am sorry, Ajay. But we cannot be together."

"I will not let you go. I can't let you go. Listen, let's elope. We will get married in some remote city and return as a married couple."

"No, Ajay. It won't work. You don't know my father. He will make our lives hell if I don't agree to this marriage. Not only mine but that of my mother and brother as well. I cannot be so selfish."

"Don't you think we deserve to live the life we want? Are we not adults now? Can't we decide how we want to live our life?"

"Ajay, you're not trying to understand."

"Make me understand, darling. Because even the thought of getting separated from you is unbearable to me. You are my life! Don't you know that?"

I'd cupped her face then and claimed her lips again. As I kissed away the salty residues of tears on her lips, she had pulled away.

"Don't be silly, Ajay. I am not your life. How long have you known me? Just these four years, right? You lived before me. You will survive without me in your life. I've to do this for my family. For you."

"I won't survive. I can't."

"Ajay, don't make it hard for me. You are a responsible adult. Not a child. Do you think your parents will be happy to see their only son wed a Christian girl? Perhaps more than my parents, they will create more barriers between us. Even if we marry, what is the guarantee that I will be accepted wholeheartedly into your family? Will they respect my beliefs or my religion? I might even be forced to convert into your religion and adopt your beliefs."

"Jasmine, you are making a lot of assumptions about the people you don't even know."

"Yes, I know I am making assumptions. But they wouldn't be far from the truth. I can't forget my family just because I fell in love. I've to think about you too. You won't understand."

"Yes. I won't understand. I don't even want to understand. But know this, Jasmine, this is a mistake. Give us one more chance. I will come to your house with my parents with a proposal."

"Don't drag your parents into this. They don't deserve that. You can't even imagine how my father would treat them."

"Okay. Then let me talk to your father now."

"Ajay, please. You shouldn't. Do you hear me? Let me make this clear. I don't want to marry you. I prefer to marry Jacob and move into a Christian family than marry a Hindu boy. I've given it a lot of thought. You will understand this as well. Hopefully soon."

She stood up and turned to walk away. Then, as if remembering something, she returned.

"Don't try to contact me ever again. I won't allow my future to be tainted by a silly affair I had in college." She'd placed her wedding invitation in my lap, along with the promise ring, and walked away.

Stunned by her callous treatment of our love, I sat numb for a long time staring at the promise ring. By the time I returned to the college auditorium where the graduation ceremony was being held, she had left.

True to her word, she had cut off all communication with me. She was not on social media anymore. She had changed her mobile number as well.

Even after all that, I hoped she would call me and tell me that it was all a mistake. I continued to apply for jobs in the hope that once I established myself in a career, I would be able to secure a future for us.

The joining date for my first job in Delhi and her wedding were on the same day. I left for Delhi three days before that date. Right on the day, I entered a new phase in my life, I had given up on love.

7

Jasmine

I logged in and the notifications began to inundate my phone. There were close to 6,000 messages in the civil gang alone. These guys!

As I scrolled through the seemingly unending messages, I searched for my name appearing in them. What I was looking for was if anybody had noticed my absence. I was not very active even before Ajay's entry. But was I such an insignificant part of the group?

Today, Ashima and Avinash were arguing about some controversial statement made by some local politician whom Ashima adored. Ajay had taken Ashima's side even though the said politician didn't deserve their support. That man was clearly aiming for a cabinet berth in the next election. But they seemed to be the minority. Avinash was being supported by almost all the others.

I typed my usual message when I became tired of their political dramas.

ME: Hey guys! Why are you wasting your time arguing over these stupid politicians?

Even during college, I had never taken any real interest in campus politics. Ajay was the left-wing party representative and he had become the Chairman of the college union in the third year as well. I had supported him then only because he was my friend.

The next moment, Ajay replied to my comment.

AJAY: Why do you interfere if you're not interested? We are having a healthy discussion here. Nobody asked for your opinion.

His first-ever direct communication with me after years! Anger bubbled inside me. There was no need for such a personal attack. A few others replied to me in the same vein, encouraged by Ajay's rudeness.

So, I replied.

ME: Just because a few of you are politically active, should we dive into all the muck that goes on in the world? There are multiple things we can discuss other than politics.

Ajay quoted my message and replied immediately.

AJAY: Oh, very well. Do tell us what we should discuss. Should we talk about the idiosyncrasies of our spouses/ partners instead? Maybe you can start by talking about your husband then. Isn't Mr Jacob interested in politics?

My whole body froze. Wasn't he aware? But was there anyone who didn't know about it? Was he mocking me?

I turned off my mobile data and threw the phone onto the couch.

I was angry with myself. Why had I asked that stupid question? I should've kept my mouth shut. I had only myself to blame for this.

My mobile began to ring with a call from Ashima. I picked it up but let it ring till it finally fell silent. I walked towards my bedroom dialling Sam's number. His number was switched off. I had momentarily forgotten that his workday must have begun there in the US. He had to deposit his phone inside a locker when he entered the factory. Sam worked in the software section of a company that manufactured defence machinery. He wouldn't be available till tomorrow morning.

I curled into a ball as painful memories started to bombard me one after the other. In reverse order.

Memories of being booed by the crowd that had gathered outside the church. The faces were blurred, but the names they called me still rang in my ears. Slut, bitch, shrew...

Then, faces started to appear in my mind's eye. The first to appear was the stunned face of Jacob. Then a face distorted by anger appeared. It was that of Jacob's mother, as she showered curses on me. Then I remembered the stony yet blank face of his father. They had been good people. They hadn't deserved the humiliation.

My mother's teary face bounced up next. Sam's face was filled with confusion. I hadn't confessed to him about Ajay or what my father had threatened to do. Somehow, I didn't remember how my father had reacted that day. Had he appeared defeated or angry? I wasn't sure. What I'd done had been unheard of in our parish. Maybe it had never happened anywhere.

Then the moments before the chaos erupted danced past.

"Do you, Jacob Augustine, in the name of God take Jasmine Emmanuel as your lawfully wedded wife?"

"I do."

Then the vicar had turned to me to repeat the question.

"Do you, Jasmine Emmanuel, in the name of God take Jacob Augustine as your husband?"

"No, I don't."

Stunned, the vicar had repeated the question two more times. Each time I answered with a no even after my father moved and stood right next to me and glared at me. His attempts to intimidate me didn't work. My mother had started to wail.

I'd felt triumphant. But those feelings immediately got drowned in the indignation that was directed at me from all directions.

"How could you?" That was the main question.

How could I? I still don't know how I'd found the courage to do that. But I'd decided to fight for our love. A desperate final attempt.

Would I have done all that if I had known this was how Ajay was going to turn out in future? Or had I turned him into this frosty individual?

I couldn't say. As bitter tears rolled down my cheeks, I tried to summon happy memories. Memories where Ajay had loved me unconditionally. Memories where Ajay had spoken only lovingly to me. They didn't come. Perhaps, just like Ajay, even his memories were refusing to give heed to my pleas.

8

Ajay

I was a jerk. What was I thinking? I shouldn't have lashed out at Jasmine. But I'd wanted to make her feel the hurt that I still felt deep inside. I was still pining for her while she had moved on and married that Jacob guy.

Ashima had DMed me privately by quoting my reply to Jasmine.

Why did you do that?

I didn't respond. I knew I'd acted rudely. I hadn't insulted her or called her a cheater, which she was. It was I who deserved all the sympathy. Not she. Ashima had sent a few angry faces as well and said that I deserved a good thrashing.

When I was contemplating as to why she was making it such a big issue, Avinash called.

"What is wrong with you, dude? Why did you reply that way to Jasmine? She is just recovering from depression."

Depression? Was that husband of hers treating her like trash? Was he giving her a hard time? Why was she depressed?

"Depressed? What happened? I thought she was happily married."

"What? Didn't you know about her wedding?"

"No. What is there to know? I left two days before her wedding. I haven't been in touch with any of you since then."

God, was something seriously wrong with her marriage? Even through my bouts of sadness and anger, I had only wished her happiness. I'd even written down her name with Jacob's surname on her wedding card before finally burning it.

"Okay. Fine. I'm driving now. I will come to your place in a few hours. Just know that you have to apologise to her."

Avinash had hung up, leaving me to ponder about all the worst-case scenarios.

Was Jacob mentally unstable or an alcoholic?

Had his actions driven Jasmine into depression?

Or was their marriage going through troubled times?

Did Jasmine have a miscarriage? I had seen a batchmate's wife undergo depression after suffering a miscarriage.

Avinash lived just two hours away from my place. He had messaged he would come and visit before I left for Delhi. After all, I hadn't returned home in years. And now he was hurrying to visit me. Something really bad must have happened to Jasmine. Had her husband died?

Two hours later when Avinash reached my place, I had almost worn out the rug of our living room thin by pacing. And then my mother had lots to ask him, so had my father. And then it was dinner time. By the time dinner was over, I'd lost all my patience. I dragged him to my room ignoring the puzzled looks of my parents.

"Tell. You are killing me with your silence."

"But you deserve this silence. After all, you've been silent all for the past five years."

"Come on, Avinash. Tell me. What's wrong with Jasmine?"

"Before that I want you to confess that you were both in love with each other while in college. All this desperation that I sense in you can only be caused by unrequited love. I had my doubts then but I had no proof. But the way you two have been carrying on ever since you became a member of the group, I know something is there. Confess, dude. Else I'm not telling you anything."

I had all the mind to beat him within an inch of his life. But he had already leaned back in the chair and crossed his arms as if ready to hear everything. So, I relented.

"Yes, we became lovers in the sixth semester, after our last class tour. We wanted to marry. But her father caught us together and even put me behind bars. Then she said she was giving in to his demands and left me hanging to marry that Jacob guy."

Avinash glowered at me.

"Oh, so it's all that pent-up frustration that you are unloading on her now. But idiot, she doesn't deserve that. She refused to marry Jacob, right in front of the vicar and a hundred guests."

A gasp escaped me.

"And that was only the beginning. She was trolled on social media for weeks because of a video taken by a guest at the wedding. Her life became a living hell. Somehow, she picked herself up and made a new life for herself in Bangalore. You don't deserve her, dude. She did all that for you. And what have you done?"

I crumpled into my bed and punched the pillow repeatedly to release my frustration. What had I done? In my haste to escape my sorrow, had I plunged the one I loved most into the wells of despair?

"I want to meet her. I can't wait to tell her how much I love her. My poor darling."

"Your poor darling? What about Anjali?"

"Anjali is just a figment of my imagination. I don't even know anyone named Anjali. She's just something my ego created to keep up the pretence that all was well in my life."

"So, there is no Anjali?"

"No, I made her up. I lied to you all."

"You scoundrel, how could you? And why?"

"Maybe I just wanted to make Jasmine jealous. Make her regret her decision of marrying Jacob."

"But you just made her all the more depressed."

"I will apologise. Now itself."

I called her, but the call wouldn't connect.

"It is like that. Either her phone will be switched off or she will not answer our call. I miss the old Jasmine. Her behaviour is quite weird most of the time. She goes without contact for days together, is always gloomy and never very active in the group," said Avinash.

I felt increasingly miserable with every word he uttered. I sent her a long message apologising for my rudeness and wishing to meet. But she didn't respond.

I decided then and there to fight for her affection once more.

I declared the same to Avinash.

"Okay, dude. Keep trying. We will find a solution to this. But promise me you will stop acting like a douchebag. After all, you are going to be in charge of the lives of a lot of people soon."

Avinash gave me a man-hug and left after reassuring me.

I tried calling Jasmine again in the next few days. Every time, the result was the same. Perhaps she used another number. A work number.

But even if I could somehow manage to get that, would she talk to me?

My heart was saying she would. Hadn't she gone against the whole world for our love?

I opened the inner chamber of my cupboard and pulled out the small jewellery box. I emptied it onto my palm. The two promise rings. She had returned her ring to me and I had continued to hold onto it like a besotted fool. I took out the ring she had given me and slipped it onto my left ring finger. It was back where it belonged.

We deserved another chance, didn't we?

9

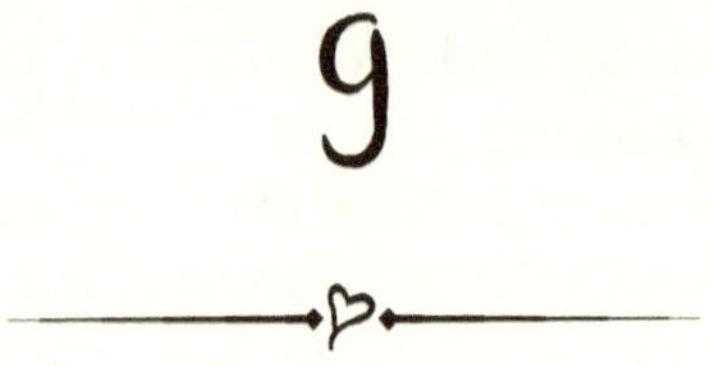

Jasmine

I continued in my escapist mode for the whole of the next week. It had taken me days to get over the hurt imparted by Ajay's words. I had not gone online after that and had avoided answering calls from Avinash and Ashima.

Thursday took me wandering to the outskirts of Bangalore inspecting the site of the new project we were beginning. This time I was in charge of the entire project and not just the structural design part. A good thing in a way. But I preferred being cooped up in front of the computer to dealing with the many headaches that a site visit brought.

As expected, meetings to solve some of the outstanding issues with the landowners took up most of the time. On Friday, it was consultation time with the geological experts. Though the area appeared arid, they had predicted that groundwater was just a few metres below the surface, making the site perfect for the apartment complexes we were constructing. The entire day passed with them moving around the site doing experiments. Their predictions were found to be accurate. Water was indeed available at the site in abundance. We rejoiced.

By evening, I had attended almost a hundred calls. My private phone sounded as the sun slowly sank behind the distant hills. I absentmindedly swiped the answer icon even without checking who it was.

When a male voice addressed me in Malayalam at the other end, I shuddered for a moment thinking it was Ajay. But it was Avinash.

"Girl, you are becoming an expert at escaping without notice. Where were you all these days? And why weren't you answering my calls?"

"Sorry. I was caught up in work," I lied.

"Oh, were you? Fine. I am coming to Bangalore this Sunday. Can we meet?"

"Let's meet," I said, agreeing to his proposal impulsively. We had last met five years ago. I definitely wanted to see him again. The only thing that worried me was how much his presence would remind me of Ajay.

We talked for about half an hour but we didn't talk about Ajay. His name came to the tip of my tongue multiple times and I quickly swallowed it. But when I thought we had exhausted almost all possible topics, Avinash asked, "What is it with you both?"

I remained silent even though I had understood who he was referring to.

"First you went MIA and now he has done the same. Perhaps I shouted at him a bit too much the other day," he said.

"You shouted at him?" I asked tentatively.

"Yes. He had no right being rude to you that way in the group. I know how much you have suffered all these years. And he had no right to say such things to you. Especially in the group. People would misunderstand."

Was that anything new to me? I seemed to attract weird reactions from people. People often made asinine assumptions about me.

"Thanks for doing that. But anyway, it is all in the past. I can't think of anything beyond work nowadays. Hey, got to go. Let's meet on Sunday then."

"Sure. Will call you with details tomorrow then."

Avinash's call put me back into Ajay-mode. I began thinking about him obsessively.

Sam called that evening just to enquire how I was faring. I had been near breaking point when he had called me the morning after Ajay had been rude to me. From then on, Sam had started calling me thrice a day to check on me. He wanted me to update him either via calls or messages if anything new was happening.

Tentatively, I told him about the proposed meeting with Avinash.

"Do you really want to do this? Meeting anyone from your class is sure to trigger memories. I hope you understand what I mean."

I knew exactly what he meant. It would trigger an avalanche of memories because Avinash and Ajay were like Siamese twins in college. You couldn't find one without the other. But I had to do this. I shouldn't shut out the world just because one person chose to throw me out of his world.

Saturday passed without a single message from Avinash. Maybe he had cancelled his trip. I felt disappointed. Was it because I wanted to see him or was it because I was hoping to hear more about Ajay from him?

Sunday morning dawned and the first thing I checked was my phone. No message from Avinash. An involuntary sigh escaped me. As I was putting the phone back on my bedside table, it rang. Avinash. I answered the phone with a smile.

"Girl, sorry. Couldn't call you yesterday. Had some last-minute meetings and stuff. Just landed in Bangalore now. Can we meet at the food court of Mantri mall today at two?" he asked.

I agreed immediately as I hadn't made any plans for the day. It was with a song playing in the back of my head that I completed my morning walk that day. Once I returned home, as I washed my face, my haggard reflection made me feel guilty. There were black rings around my eyes, my skin looked pale and sheen-less and my hair was a mess. After breakfast, I applied oil to my hair, applied a face pack, and took a long warm shower. By the time I began getting ready, I didn't look heartbroken. I looked completely healed, even though every breath still felt heavy.

I reached the mall thirty minutes late, owing to an unexpected traffic jam along my route. I had stepped on the escalator when my phone rang.

"Hey, are you coming?" Avinash asked. He appeared to have lost all patience.

"Yes, I am almost there. Where are you seated?" I asked.

"Come to the area in front of the Subway kiosk. I am waiting."

Does the heart have some special sense of knowing when a loved one is near? Maybe it does, because my heart suddenly started to leap and bounce like a happy toddler. Its behaviour made sense when I saw a familiar figure seated across from Avinash. Ajay! He had his back to me, but I would recognise him even amid a crowd of thousands.

My first impulse was to turn and flee. But then I steeled myself and walked forward. It was better to get this over with. If he could move on, why couldn't I? Even though my legs weighed like lead, I dragged myself to where they were seated.

"Surprise!" said Avinash when he saw me. "Look who decided to join us at the last moment."

I smiled as if the surprise didn't overwhelm me. I sat on the empty chair next to Avinash after shaking hands with both. The moment Ajay held my hand, I melted from within. I hadn't forgotten how warm his hands were. The warmth prodded out a thousand memories and I blinked back the tears that were forming at the back of my eyes. And the worst of it all, he looked as breathtakingly handsome as always.

"How are you, Jasmine? Where do you work?" asked Ajay.

Hearing his voice and feeling his gaze on me made me nervous like a mouse. My knees started to tremble. I was grateful we were seated. What I answered, I still don't remember.

Surprisingly, Ajay, who was always eloquent, didn't speak much after that. He did look at me a lot, that much I knew even though I tried to avoid looking in his direction. He seemed lost in thought as Avinash made jokes and singlehandedly made sane conversation.

When the waiter came to take our order, Ajay and I said at the same time, "I want mixed fried rice." Our eyes met and held. I was the first one to look away. I felt Ajay's eyes on me even as Avinash joked about wanting to order everything on the menu.

Mixed fried rice was something we both loved. This variant of fried rice had been our favourite during college days. It was a delicious mixture of every single non-veg and veg ingredient that was usually used for making fried rice. Egg, prawns, chicken, mushroom, carrot...you name it, you would find it. Over the years whenever I ate mixed fried rice, invariably my thoughts wandered to Ajay.

Did he still love fruit salad with chocolate ice cream? He did. I heard him order fruit salad for himself. I also ordered the same. It felt like being back in college.

Blood crept to my cheeks and I couldn't raise my eyes to meet Ajay's even when I knew he was looking at me during our conversation. This wasn't going well. I was going to make myself a fool and launch myself into his arms. And he would humiliate me again.

We were in the middle of lunch when a text from Sam landed on my phone.

"Jazz, I am in front of your apartment. Where are you?"

He was in Bangalore. The sly fellow. He hadn't talked about travelling here when we had talked last morning. He had, in fact, told me he was going to attend a conference and wouldn't be available on phone till today evening. So, this was his conference. I rolled my eyes and smiled. Then texted back.

"I am at Mantri mall. I told you na, meeting Avinash. And guess who came with him?"

"Shit. I am coming there. Wait. I am coming to rescue you. I will be there in 15." His message came the next moment even though I hadn't mention Ajay's name.

Maybe that would be better.

"Don't come in. Call me when you reach here." I didn't want him to meet Ajay.

This meeting was proving to be more painful with each passing second. I missed the old Ajay. The person in front of me was just a shadow of the person who had been madly in love with me. He didn't seem interested in me. Whenever I looked, he was mostly bartering glances with Avinash as if silently making an escape plan.

But this time, when I looked up from the phone, I found Ajay's eyes fixed on my phone. His curiosity seemed to have been piqued. Yet, he didn't utter a word. His silence was killing me.

After lunch, we continued to sit and talk, Avinash leading the way. He urged me to talk about my latest project. I struggled just to put words together to create a coherent sentence. Words refused to flow. I stuttered and my thoughts scattered because now Ajay's eyes were again focussed on my face.

When I was in the middle of describing our current venture, I noticed something shining on Ajay's left ring finger. A plain silver ring. Was it the promise ring I had given him?

I forgot what I was saying. An awkward silence danced around us. Though I wanted to ask if it was the same ring, I dreaded the answer. It could be a different one. Maybe Anjali had gifted it to him.

Avinash glanced at me, puzzled at my silence, and then at Ajay. He stood up and declared he had to use the washroom urgently. Ajay smiled at Avinash as if he wanted him to vanish as soon as possible. I swallowed. I realized I didn't want to be left alone with Ajay. Once alone, he was surely going to tell me that he had moved on. Or brag about Anjali. Or say that I deserved what I went through. Or insult me. I might not survive any of that.

Luckily, Sam called just then. I answered at the first ring, told him I was coming out and I stood up immediately.

"I've got to go, guys. It was nice meeting you," I shook hands with both and fled from the food court.

It was only when I launched myself into Sam's arms that I finally breathed in relief. He hugged me tight and we got into the waiting taxi. As I looked towards the mall, I saw

Ajay stationed at the entrance, staring in our direction.

I wished I could just run into his arms. But now there was an invisible wall between us. Her name was Anjali.

53

10

Ajay

My body tensed as I watched Jasmine run into the arms of a handsome young man. My chest constricted and it became difficult to breathe. I was jolted back to reality when she happily accompanied the stranger into the waiting cab. Nervous energy flushed through my whole body and I summoned the first auto that came my way. I jumped in and asked the auto driver to follow Jasmine's cab.

To see her within an arm's reach after all these years had felt surreal, almost unbearably happy. I had become tongue-tied the moment she appeared before me. As the minutes had ticked past, I had tried everything to make myself talk. But guilt, sadness and desperation had kept my words confined to a few polite enquiries.

There had been moments when I had wanted to just reach out and pull her into my arms. There had been moments when I had wanted to kneel before her and apologise for having kept myself away from her all these years.

Avinash had promised to leave us alone at an appropriate moment. I had been mentally writing a long speech to apologise after Avinash declared he had to use the restroom when she suddenly stood up and declared that she was leaving. After remaining indecisive for a few minutes, thinking about whether or not to follow her, I dashed after her only to find her run into the arms of a man.

Had I lost her yet another time?

The voice of the auto driver ended my reverie just then.

"Sir, they've stopped. Do I stop as well?" The taxi had stopped in front of an apartment complex.

"Yes, stop."

I sat in the auto and waited for Jasmine to emerge from their taxi. When she came out, she was still holding on to the arm of the stranger, her face bright with happiness. Who was this man? My blood boiled. I wanted to punch him. I wasn't ready to believe that after all she had done for our love, she had moved on.

I followed them and rushed into the lift after them. Jasmine gasped.

"What are you doing here? You followed me?"

"Yes, I did. Who is he?" I asked as the bespectacled young man directed a bored gaze at me.

"None of your business," said Jasmine and moved to the corner of the lift.

"Really, Jazz? None of his business? It's definitely his business. Ajay, right? I'm Sam, Jasmine's brother," said the young man and extended his hand toward me.

I felt like a loser as I shook his hand. When did the scrawny teenager that I had met occasionally while in college transform into this dapper young man? He told me he was currently on-site in the US for a project.

"I had to dash down to Bangalore because my sister has been down in the dumps for the last few weeks. I have come to cheer her up," he said, tossing a loving glance at Jasmine.

Jasmine stood silent even as Sam continued to talk about her, her face devoid of any emotion. Was she angry that I had followed her?

When we reached the fourth floor, Jasmine got out first and I followed her. Sam stayed put inside the lift.

"You guys should talk. I left my luggage at the airport hotel. Will get it and be back in two hours."

I smiled at him gratefully.

"Remember, two hours only, okay?" he said and winked at me just as the lift doors closed.

Jasmine opened the main door to her apartment, pushed it open and waved me in. Once I walked in, she closed the door and leaned against it, her gaze fixed on me.

"What do you want, Ajay? Why are you here?" she asked. The pain in her voice tugged at my heart.

"Do you have to ask that, Jasmine? I am still in love with you. I want you in my life. I want us back. Can we forget the past five years?"

"How can we? It is too late. You have Anjali now."

"There is no Anjali. Do you hear? I lied. I am sorry. I thought I had to act as if I had moved on too."

Jasmine pushed away from the door and approached me.

"Is that true?" she asked when she was just a hand's length away from me.

I nodded.

With a groan, she rained punches on my chest. I laughed out loud in relief.

This was what she used to do when she was mad at me while in college. I grabbed her arms and held them imprisoned behind her exactly the way I used to do back then. And then I kissed her. I kissed her as if my life depended on it. Softly, she surrendered to me and her petal-like lips blossomed, inviting me to explore. When we finally emerged from that kiss, her cheeks were wet with tears.

"Am I that bad a kisser?" I teased, wiping her tears and dropping a kiss on her forehead.

"You are. But still, I love you," she whispered. She started sobbing uncontrollably and I held her till the sobs died down. Then I led her to the couch and made her sit. I walked into the kitchen and fetched a glass of water for Jasmine. I fondly watched her as she drained the glass swiftly.

"Sorry, darling. I shouldn't have barged in on you like this. But I thought I'd lost you again when I saw Sam embrace you," I said and caressed her cheeks.

"Were you jealous?"

"No," I lied.

"You were."

"I was," I accepted with a smile.

It was the truth. Jealousy had been my constant companion for years. Until Jasmine had confessed her love to me. Till then, I'd wanted to beat every single boy who laid an eye on her. I had loitered about her like any insecure lover would when he wasn't sure of his success.

Jasmine caught my palm and touched the promise ring on my finger.

"You kept it. I thought you would've thrown it away."

"I couldn't. You were my warmest sorrow. I couldn't part with your memories or thoughts about you. I tried. By God, I tried."

"I tried too. But couldn't. I love you a hundred times more now than I loved you then."

"Yes, darling. I feel the same. Wait. I have something of yours," I said and took out her promise ring from my purse.

A smile brightened her face and she eagerly extended her left hand toward me. My heart felt as if it would explode with joy when I finally saw it shining brightly on her finger.

"I promise I will replace it with something prettier soon. But promise me you will not leave again," I said as I pulled her closer.

"I won't if you convince me that you love me as much as before." The mischievous glitter in her eyes made me grin. She wound her arms around my neck and bit my ear playfully. "Ready to prove it, my hero?"

Her words fell on my ears like honey. I dipped my head and claimed her lips. Our lips tangled and my arms wandered down her back to cup her bottom. She moaned and pressed closer. I was now fully aroused. I could sense that she wanted me too. Blissful memories from a long-ago weekend assaulted my senses, heightening my desire. I picked her up in my arms and asked, "Which one is the bedroom?"

She pointed at the second door in the hall with a shy smile and hid her head in the crook of my shoulder.

I had dreamt about this moment for so long. It all felt unreal now that it was finally coming true.

My lips never left hers as I walked happily with the best blessing God had bestowed on me. She felt wonderful and her lips tasted like the chocolate ice cream we'd had after lunch. Years of longing and desire made me shiver in anticipation as I pushed the door to her bedroom open. Laying her on the bed, I hovered over her and claimed her lips again and again. It felt heavenly to feel her warmth against me.

Jasmine shivered and clasped the hair on my nape as I dragged my palm to cup her breast. With a groan, I covered her mouth with mine, determined to steal her breath with every nip and caress. She pressed herself against me and exhaled deeply, letting her head fall back on the pillow.

When I tasted the sensitive flesh of her neck and kissed the throbbing pulse at the hollow of her throat, she cupped my face and looked deep into my eyes.

"Tell me this isn't a dream, Ajay."

"It isn't, my darling. This time, we are together, never to part again. I will promise you that."

"Mark me as yours then, Ajay. Claim every inch of me as yours," she said softly, as her fingers frantically worked to unbutton my shirt.

Who was I to deny her request? I was eager to please and she seemed determined to be happy.

All was well in my world again.

11

Jasmine

Life had never felt so good.

I can't believe I married Ajay, the love of my life, today.

I can't believe that he had stormed back into my world just a month ago.

It had only taken us a few minutes to forgive each other. The sadness accumulated from the years apart had melted away within hours. I had transformed from the depressed, insecure girl who had lost the love of her life to the girl who was happily in love. Once again.

The man I loved had forced himself into my life and changed my life overnight. He had done everything from then on to make me happy.

I had told Ajay that I didn't care whether or not my family approved of our relationship. I just wanted us to be together. But somehow, he had sensed that deep within my heart, I yearned for their approval. I did miss my family. He knew that the one thing I had been passionate about before everything went wrong had been my family. He had been to my home enough times to understand that though my father was insufferably strict, he loved me. I had been his favourite child.

In a way, our love affair had torn the family apart. If I hadn't fallen in love, I might have married the man they'd chosen for me. I would have perhaps remained the darling of my parents. I wouldn't have felt like an outcast.

So, the first thing he did the day after we met was to recruit Sam into his team. When I left for the office reluctantly the next morning, they had been immersed in a serious discussion regarding our future.

"I want you guys to be together. I can't see my sister suffer like this ever again. My father is stubborn. But he will see the error of his ways. But anyway, when he knows you have become an IAS officer now, he will become a progressive father who doesn't care about religion or his pride."

I had chuckled hearing Sam say those words. The rest of the day had passed in a blur as I had back to back meetings all day long. By the time I got back, they were making plans to travel. To Kerala. Without me. I wouldn't hear any of it and had accompanied them.

Our reception at home had been cold initially. But everything went exactly as Sam had predicted. My father indeed had a weakness for powerful people. And he had liked Ajay when he was just my friend. Altogether, Ajay won him over without much difficulty. Ajay was not the meek college graduate now. He was an amazing bureaucrat who could win any argument, or turn any discussion his way. In every way, he was perfect. My chest swelled with pride noting the changes in the youth I had fallen in love with. Soon, they were discussing politics, bureaucracy and everything under the sun. Sam winked at me. My mother's face lit up with a smile.

All my apprehensions about Ajay's family not accepting me also got tossed into the wind the very next day. His mother had embraced me like her own daughter and so had his father. When his mother slid a golden bangle onto my right arm, claiming me as family, there hadn't been a dry eye in the room.

Our relatives had been a different story. Some of them rejoiced that they had a high up bureaucrat as their relative now. But a few declared that as Ajay was the reason I had humiliated them all in front of society, he wasn't welcome into their homes. As if that was a punishment! Sam had called it a blessing.

And according to the wishes of both families, we had two weddings today. First, according to Hindu rituals and the second, a Christian wedding. I became a bride twice. How many had the privilege of getting married like that?

I was nervous throughout the Hindu wedding ceremony. But it helped that it was not as elaborate or complicated as the Christian wedding rituals.

Ajay had joked later that south Indian Hindu wedding ceremonies lasted for a shorter period than the time it took to finish eating the wedding feast.

For the Hindu wedding, I had been attired in a scarlet red silk sari with gold thread embroidery and for the Christian ceremony, I had chosen an A-line gown with delicate lace and ribbon work. I loved the way Ajay's eyes lit up when he saw me as a bride, both times. His eyes had become misty when he saw me walking down the aisle holding onto my father's arm. And in answer, my own eyes had misted.

Ajay's niece, an adorable five-year-old, had won my heart when she ran to me and hugged me tightly. Then she had asked, "Are you a princess?"

When I said no, she asked who I was. I told her I was her new aunt. Her hands had flown to her lips in astonishment.

Then she had told everyone who listened that she was going to get married one day wearing that very gown. Such a darling!

"You look like jasmine now. Delicate and pure. I am happy that I married you twice. Maybe we should renew our vows every year." Ajay had whispered in my ears when he carried me across the threshold of my new home.

I would happily marry him any number of times. In every incarnation I took on this planet, I want to be only his.

According to Ajay, his warmest sorrow had finally transformed into eternal bliss. Our bliss.

THE END

Author's Note

When I first wrote it, Ajay's and Jasmine's story was difficult to put down on paper as I was going through some personal issues. This story was initially published as part of the Anthology "Something Old, Something New," which is no longer on Amazon. I had initially thought of expanding it a bit but somehow, even though I tweaked it a bit here and there, Ajay's and Jasmine's story seemed complete. Those of you who might have read the anthology might have noticed that I took the liberty to change the female lead's name.

If you liked their story, do tell me about it.

You can write to me at authorpreethi@gmail.com

Please do not forget to leave reviews on Amazon and Goodreads. Reviews matter a lot to us authors.

You can find me on Instagram and Twitter @preethivenu

Thank you,

Preethi Venugopala

Acknowledgements

This story was initially published as part of the Anthology "Something Old, Something New," which is no longer on Amazon. Writing on a theme that too in a time-bound manner was difficult. I was dealing with some personal issues but my group of writer buddies kept cheering me up and giving just the right prods when required. If not for them, this story wouldn't have been written. So, thank you to my amazing writing pals. Cheers to all of you! Aarti, Shilpa, Andaleeb, Debdutta, Ruchi, Devika... you girls rock!

As always, a BIG thank you to my dear husband Venugopala and my son Akshaj for being my cheerleaders. I love you both.

Bestselling author Reet Singh was kind enough to do a quick beta reading and provided some very valuable feedback. Thank you, Reet for your X-ray vision and constant support.

A big thank you to my editor Nikita Jhanglani who always does a commendable job.

Thank you, God, for helping me find happiness through writing.

Lastly, thank you, dear reader, for picking this book. You are my favourite person in the world.

Preethi Venugopala

SREEPURAM SERIES
Book 1: The Girl at the Wedding

A Sweet Romance Novella about Arranged Marriages, Family and Love.

Kishore is home on vacation after three years. To his horror, his family is determined to get him married this time. He creates the perfect plan to escape the matchmaking attempts of his family. Just when he thought he had everything under control, a girl from his past literally crashes into his life and turns his life upside down. Within a day, he is ready to sacrifice his bachelorhood entranced by the girl he meets at his friend's wedding.
One misstep and he acquire a rival. His own cousin, Abhishek.
What can he do to win back the love of his life?
Shreya can't believe that the handsome young man she is slowly falling in love with is the bully she hated in school. He has transformed in every possible way. She likes everything about him. But then something happens that prompts her to make a rash decision.

Would this one decision ruin her chances of finding true love?

Or would she have the courage to fight for love?

Book 2: Without You

Dr Arjun enters Ananya's life like a whirlwind, bringing with him the spirit of young love.

Does the path of true love ever run smooth?
Circumstances force them apart even though they were irrevocably in love. She becomes a victim of depression. When everything fails to return her to normalcy, help

arrives from an unexpected source.
Will she ever find happiness again?

Will time allow her heart to heal and forget Arjun?

What indeed is true love?

What is that strange secret that locks all the circumstances together?

Travel with Ananya to the picturesque Sreepuram, face the chaos of Bengaluru, and relish the warmth of magical Dubai in this heart-warming tale of love, betrayal, friendship, and miracles.

Book 3: His Sunshine Girl

Can two damaged souls heal each other?

Shalini is dusky and has faced body shaming throughout her life because of it. She has gone through a lot in her life, including a failed marriage and divorce, and is at a crossroad when the story begins.

She arrives in Sreepuram as the live-in literary assistant to Arundhati Mukundan, an eminent author.

Dr.Vishal, Arundhati's grandson and a pediatrician, has seen love and loss at close quarters.

When they meet in Sreepuram, it is a reunion of two childhood friends who were once inseparable.

Will their friendship help them heal?

Isn't friendship turning into love the most beautiful thing on earth?

Would fate allow that to happen or would it play its devious role again?

This is a standalone sequel to the best seller 'Without You'. You can read this even if you haven't read 'Without You.'

This story picks up from where 'Without You' ended.

Look out for some of your favourite characters from 'Without You' taking on significant roles in this story.

SRAVANAPURA ROYAL SERIES
Book 1: A Royal Affair

A British commoner in love with an Indian Prince

When Jane Worthington, a reporter with a London based entertainment channel, comes to India she is sure of two things.

Firstly, she would find Daniel Worthington, the lost twin of her beloved Grandfather and fulfill his last wish.

Secondly, now that she was in India, she was not going to think about Prince Vijay Dev Varman, the scion of the erstwhile royal family of Sravanapura, the man who broke her heart years ago.

Two seemingly impossible tasks.

Vijay always believed he knew everything about himself and his family. But when Jane storms back into his life, secrets tumble out one after the other disturbing the very thread of discipline that had granted his life a semblance of sanity.

Jane cannot refuse Vijay's offer of help but every moment with him is a torture because he is not the carefree youth she had once fallen in love with.

Will they succeed to find Daniel Worthington when every single trace of his existence seems to have been carefully wiped off by unseen hands?

Or will their quest reveal secrets that will make it impossible for them to even dream of a happily ever after?

A Suspense Novella about Second Chances in Love

Book 2: he Princess and the Superstar

A Princess in love with a Bollywood Superstar

Saketh Rao aka SR, India's latest Bollywood heartthrob, has bagged the role of a lifetime: to play Hari Varman, the doomed royal scion.

When he arrives at Sravanapura Palace with his director friend Rajeev Ratnam, little does he know that his life is about to change forever!

Princess Kritika is overjoyed that Saketh Rao will play the role of her ancestor. But when she comes face to face with the arrogant superstar she is determined to scuttle the project.

Fate, however, has different plans for them. The feisty couple is soon head over heels in love with each other.

As they uncover the secrets of Hari Varman's life, Saketh makes a discovery that can rip them apart and their new-found love.

Will the secrets and lies of the past deny them a future together?

Or will they overcome the obstacles to love?

Book 3: The Lost Princess

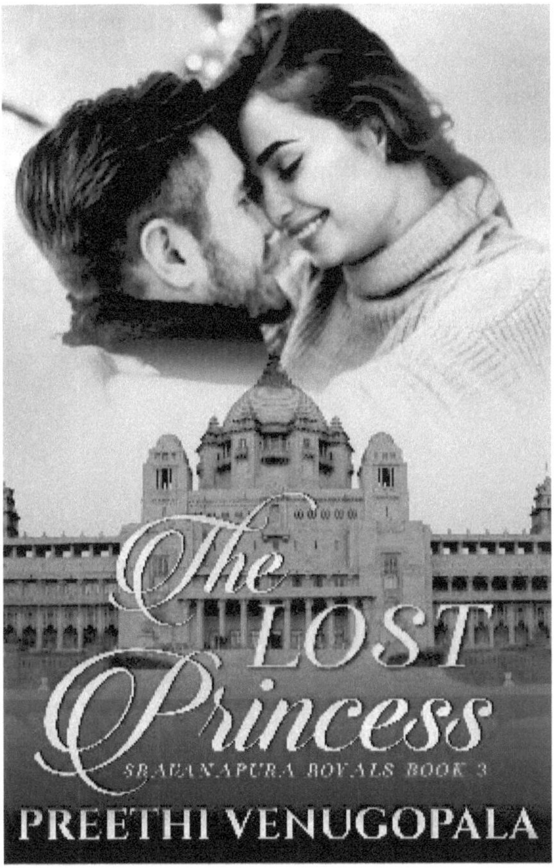

HOW FAR WOULD YOU GO TO PROTECT THE ONE YOU LOVE?

Ishaani, the newly crowned nightingale of the Indian music industry has it all: a dream career, a loving family and loyal friends. Yet, the man she has loved all her life will not warm up to her.

Rajeev, a hotshot movie director, has feelings for Ishaani. But, she is his sister's best friend and has been like another sibling to him. Yet, what can he do if he feels compelled to make her his own?

Then, Ishaani's life changes overnight. She is no longer a lowly commoner but a princess.

She has to make some tough decisions to protect the man she loves.

Her choices lead them both down a path filled with shocking revelations and devastating consequences.

Will true love prevail?

Or will the many twists of fate tear them apart?

Book 4: Love and Longing in Firefly Season

Rashi Ratnam, the newly minted design assistant of **billionaire fashion designer** Neel Mishra, is sceptical when she leaves on a field trip to Kerala with her temperamental boss.

It doesn't matter that she has been harbouring a crush on her gorgeous boss since forever.

The man intimidates her and is cold like ice.

Also, he hasn't still forgotten his ex-girlfriend.

At **Heaven's Cove**, the beautiful backwater island owned by Neel's grandparents, Rashi begins to see Neel in a new light. She also discovers his best-kept secrets.

It is the **firefly season**, and there is nothing that stops her from falling madly in love with Neel.

But **love** is not easy.

With Neel's jealous ex-girlfriend hovering around them stirring up troubles, life becomes strenuous.

Can they face the curve balls that fate throws at them?

Or will their love die a slow death?

But in the end, is the choice theirs to make?

Read this heartwarming contemporary love story of letting go and letting love in.

P.S: This book can also be read as a standalone romance. So, you can read this even if you haven't read the Sravanapura Royals series.

Remember When

A Passionate Love Story with the Chennai Floods 2015 as Backdrop

Dedicated to the volunteers who kept Chennai afloat during the floods

On the outside, Tara leads a perfect life. A home of her own, a handsome husband, a doting son and a promising career as an author.

But inside, she is a wreck. Her marriage is a sham and she hasn't succeeded in forgetting her one true love, Manu, the man she had wronged. The man she had almost married.

Manu, now the senior editor with a science portal, firmly believes that he has left Tara where she belonged: in his past. But in reality, he hasn't forgotten anything. Not the love nor the hurt.

Their past and present collide when they accidentally meet in **Chennai.** The city has come to a standstill after facing the worst **flood** in a century. While nature is unleashing its fury on humans, they must make peace with their past.

Will they have the courage to do that?

Can they fight the attraction that still burns bright?

Or will the bunch of people they are with, teach them new life lessons?

What is the secret that is burning Tara from within?

Falling for Cinderella

When what you seek is seeking you...

Karan: It all started at a masquerade ball. I took one look at the girl dressed as **Cinderella** and fell **head over heels** in love.

I was not someone who believed in love.

Yet, within a few hours, she made me crave for things I never knew I wanted.

I began to equate her presence with happiness.

Like a warm breeze on that winter night, she thawed my frozen heart.

At midnight, she ran away without telling me who she really was. Just like Cinderella.

I was never the same again.

I couldn't forget her, but she came visiting only in my dreams.

No matter what, I was determined to find her.

Chandni: Karan was not someone I could even dream about.

I was a poor orphan, a nobody.

He was a billionaire, the hottest bachelor in India, coveted by rich women everywhere.

A dance: that was all he asked.

But while we danced, I gave him my heart, knowing that the magic would end once he realized my true identity.

I was nothing but a cheat.

Yet, the **magic** didn't end that night.

A bizarre twist of fate put me in his path again. I had to hide my secret, even though I wished to confess everything to him.

Was watching him from afar the only thing that was written in my destiny?

My Warmest Sorrow

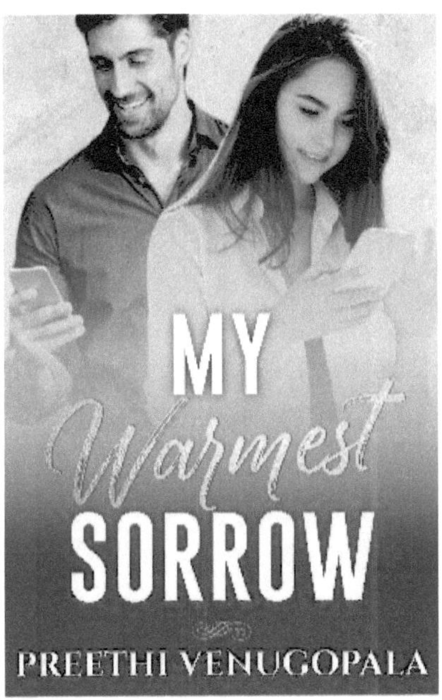

♥ **What would you do when you come face to face with your past?** ♥

Social media which is often a source of entertainment can be a source of great sorrow as well. Especially **alumni WhatsApp groups**, as not all memories are pleasant.

When Ajay, now an IAS officer, gets added to his **college** WhatsApp group, all his classmates welcome him warmly. Except for Jasmine.

Jasmine and Ajay were inseparable while in college. Their relationship had transitioned from being **best friends**

to lovers over the duration of the engineering course. But then **fate** had intervened, and they became estranged.

Five years of silence have created a **wall of sorrow** between them. Their interactions in the class WhatsApp group are nothing like what they once used to be. Every moment churns out more anguish and unpleasantness.

Jasmine is still living with the repercussions of what had happened in the **past**. Ajay's indifference throws her into despair.

What had caused their **separation**?
Is **love** still hiding underneath their public facades?
What **lies** are they concealing?

Other Works By The Author

Short Stories
A Christmas in London
My Red Knight
Kid's Books
Anya and the Spring Fairy
The Teddy who ran away
Learn Malayalam Alphabets through English